SPIRIT!
Cheer!
SQUAD!
POM!
CHEER!
FLY!
Cheer!
SQUAD!
POM
CHEER!
Yell!
CHEER!
Cheer!
SQUAD!
CHEER!
Cheer!
FLY!
CHANT!
SPIRIT!
Yell!
JUMP!

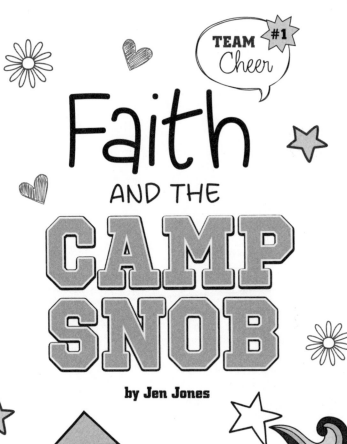

TEAM Cheer #1

Faith

AND THE

CAMP
SNOB

by Jen Jones

STONE ARCH BOOKS
a capstone imprint

Team Cheer is published by Stone Arch Books
A Capstone Imprint
151 Good Counsel Drive, P.O. Box 669
Mankato, Minnesota 56002
www.capstonepub.com

Library of Congress Cataloging-in-Publication Data
Jones, Jen.
  Faith and the camp snob / by Jen Jones.
    p. cm. — (Team Cheer)
  Summary: Faith Higgins is anxious about attending cheer camp with her team, and having to deal with her snobbish teammate Ella is not making things easier.
  ISBN-13: 978-1-4342-2994-6 (library binding)
  ISBN-10: 1-4342-2994-7 (library binding)
  1. Cheerleading—Juvenile fiction. 2. Sports camps—Juvenile fiction. 3. Middle schools—Juvenile fiction. 4. Friendship—Juvenile fiction. 5. Anxiety—Juvenile fiction. 6. Interpersonal relations—Juvenile fiction. [1. Cheerleading—Fiction. 2. Camps—Fiction. 3. Middle schools—Fiction. 4. Schools—Fiction. 5. Friendship—Fiction. 6. Anxiety—Fiction. 7. Interpersonal relations—Fiction.] I. Title.
  PZ7.J720311Fai 2011
  813.54—dc22   2011001997

Art Director: Kay Fraser
Designer: Emily Harris
Editor: Julie Gassman
Production Specialist: Michelle Biedscheid

Photo credits: Geno Nicholas, 110;
Getty Images: Digital Vision, cover, 3
Artistic Elements: Shutterstock: belle,
blue67design, Nebojsa I, notkoo

Printed in the United States of America in Stevens Point, Wisconsin.
032011   06111WZF11

TEAM #1
Cheer

Faith
AND THE
CAMP SNOB

by Jen Jones

Greenview Middle School Cheer Team Roster

NAME	GRADE
Britt Bolton	7th
Kate Ellis	7th
Gaby Fuller	8th
Sheena Hays	8th
Faith Higgins	8th
Ella Jenkins	8th

That's me! Faith Higgins, squad newbie.

Ugh! Ella drives me nuts! She is a huge part of my insecurity issues.

Gaby is a bubbly, fun girl who just happens to be my neighbor! She's the kind of friend that makes terrible things, like being the new girl at school, so much easier!

Part of my new circle of friends, Lissa is the one who will stand up for her friends, no matter what. She's feisty and fabulous!

Ella's sidekick . . . need I say more?

Kacey Kosir	8th
Melissa "Lissa" Marks	8th
Trina Mathews	8th
Brooke Perrino	8th
Mackenzie Potz	7th
Maddie Todd	7th

Coach: Bernadette Adkins

Brooke is pretty much the leader of our squad. She likes being in charge, but she is super friendly and always willing to help people, which makes her a great friend.

CHEER!
Yell!
FLY!
CHEER!
SPIRIT!
Cheer!
FLY!
CHANT!
YELL!
FLY!
Cheer!
Yell!
CHEER!
SPIRIT!
CHEER!
Squad!
SPIRIT!
SQUAD!
Jump!
SPIRIT!
Cheer!
CHEER!
SQUAD!
YELL!
Cheer!
Cheer!
Cheer!
SPIRIT!
CHANT!
CHEER!
Yell!
CHEER!
FLY!
CHEER!
FLY!
CHANT!
Cheer!
SPIRIT!
CHEER!
CHEER!
CHEER!
SQUAD!
FLY!
Cheer!
CHANT!
Jump!
CHANT!
FLY!
YELL!

Chapter 1

Picture a cheerleader. Odds are the girl who comes to mind is super perky, petite, and outgoing, right? Now picture the exact opposite of the typical pom-toting princess. You'll have a good idea of who I am. Tall and lanky, pretty shy, and hating the spotlight.

So most people would probably be surprised to learn that I was actually the newest member of the Greenview Middle School cheer squad. In fact, at the start of the school year, I was the "new girl" at school, too. Fun times. It was not a role I was excited about playing.

"Earth to Faith!" yelled Gaby Fuller, waking me up from my daydream. Gaby was my way-more-extroverted friend. She really *was* everything you'd picture a cheerleader to be. Curvy, cute, and extra bubbly, Gaby oozed enthusiasm. "You'd better snap out of it before practice starts, or Coach A is going to make you run extra laps around the gym."

"Anything but that," I joked. Even though I'd only been on the squad a short time, it was long enough to know that Coach Adkins was one tough cookie. "Those pushups and power jumps last time were bad enough. I could barely walk the next day!"

It was a hot July day, and Gaby and I were walking to cheer practice together. We lived on the same street. She was one of the very first people I met when my family moved into the neighborhood. I was really grateful for the way she'd taken me under her wing.

"Well, I'm sure today will be killer, too," said Gaby. "The last practice before camp is always hard-core."

SUMMER CAMP

AT

ROSEN COLLEGE

* Stunts
* Jumps
* Tumbling
* Dance
* Cheer

I felt butterflies flutter in my stomach at the mention of cheer camp. The last few months had been such a whirlwind. I was still wrapping my brain around even being a cheerleader, let alone going off to a camp full of them!

"I'm so glad we're rooming together," I told Gaby, smiling.

"Me, too!" she said, linking her arm with mine. "It'll be like we're bringing a slice of Spring Street to Rosen College."

I marveled silently at how Spring Street had brought us together. My mom and I had been walking home from the grocery store one day when we spotted Gaby and another cheerleader friend, Lissa Marks, practicing dance routines in Gaby's front yard.

Wheels turning, my mom struck up a conversation in hopes of helping me make some new friends. (That whole coming-out-of-my-shell thing isn't exactly my strong suit.) Ten minutes later, I'd somehow been convinced by Gaby to attend Greenview's cheerleading tryouts the next day.

"Mom, what are you thinking?" I complained as we walked away. "I'm going to humiliate myself and become the new school dork. I'm not exactly cheerleader material."

"I beg to differ," she argued. "First of all, you've always loved sports, and you're not too shabby on the dance floor, either. And should I even mention how many times I've caught you watching *Bring It On* and *Fired Up** on cable?"

She had me there. I'd always been fascinated by the fast-paced, flashy world of cheerleading. But as a spectator — not a participant. "All right, you've got a point," I agreed. "But watching it and doing it are two different things."

"Why not just try?" my mom pleaded. "It will help you meet some new people before school starts. Worse comes to worst, you can check another daring feat off the bucket list."

—————

*So I'm pretty sure you already know all about these movies. And if you don't, you are missing out. But Bring It On is about two competing cheer squads — both amazing. And Fired Up tells the story of two high school guys who go to cheer camp to meet girls. Not surprisingly, it's super funny!

The Higgens Family Bucket List

- ~~Learn how to salsa dance (Mom)~~
- Be a contestant on The Price is Right (Dad)
- Collect every He-Man figure in existence (Stevie)
- Visit every continent on Earth (Faith)
- Fly in a blimp (Stevie)
- See Mount Rushmore (Mom)
- Meet a President (Dad)
- Be in the Macy's Thanksgiving Day Parade (Faith)
- Go to a fancy awards show like the Oscars (Mom)
- Make a million dollars! (Stevie)
- Run for office (Dad)
- Milk a cow . . . or goat (Faith)
- Visit a rainforest (Dad)
- Go to a world series game (Mom)

Our "bucket list" was a running joke in our family, but it was actually one of my favorite things. We kept a giant list on the fridge of things that all of us want to do before "kicking the bucket" one day. It was a little morbid, maybe, but we all loved it! Some of the things were way offbeat, like my dad's "be a contestant on *The Price is Right*" or my brother's "collect every He-Man figure in existence." But it was still a lot of fun!

"Funny, I don't remember putting trying out for cheerleading on the list," I said. "But maybe it should be."

And sure enough, I somehow found the courage to try out the next day. Now here I was, practically BFF with Gaby and ready to rock my first real performance at cheer camp.

Gaby and I rounded the corner, and Greenview Middle School came into sight.

My nervous jitters returned as I thought about starting school in the fall. It was hard enough being shy, but the thought of being the new girl was enough to put me over the edge. I took a deep breath and tried to focus on being in the moment instead. "Hey, Gabs, I'll race you to the parking lot!" I called, getting a head start.

"Oh, it's on!" said Gaby, flying past me in a blur of ponytail. We managed a dead-even finish, collapsing in giggles as we reached the school grounds.

"Where's the fire?" I heard a voice call. It was Lissa Marks, getting out of her mom's old VW Rabbit along with our other friend, Brooke Perrino. Both cheerleaders, they were Gaby's longtime BFFs. We'd all been hanging out a lot since I'd made the team.

"Oh, it's in the gym. Didn't you hear?" teased Gaby as they approached. "After all, our camp routine is *en fuego**." Lissa was Latina, and she'd taught us lots of fun Spanish expressions. Gaby loved to put them to good use!

~~~~~~~

*en fuego = on fire, as in hot, or in the case of our camp routine, awesome! we are all hoping to do well at camp. Sure, camp is a place to learn, but we're all there to compete, too.

"You can say that again," said Brooke. "We better get Camp Champs this year."

The three of them exchanged knowing glances. I had a feeling Brooke was referring to last year, when the squad had gotten second place to our cheer rivals, Pioneer Middle School. Though I was new to all of this, I knew they were the squad to beat.

"Well, you've got a secret weapon this year," I said. "You've got . . . me!" Normally, I wouldn't put myself out there so much, but my new friends gave me a boost of confidence.

"You better believe it," said Gaby, doing a ***Charlie's Angels**** pose and playfully blowing smoke from an imaginary gun. "They're not gonna know what hit 'em."

"Here's to Faith!" said Brooke, holding up her hand for a high-five. I hoped no one would notice that I was glowing

---

*You might know <u>Charlie's Angels</u> as the two movies starring Drew Barrymore, Cameron Diaz, and Lucy Liu as three high-kicking, supersmart crime fighters. But it was also a TV show back in the late '70s—early '80s. It's good for some retro fun!

with happiness. Kind of nerdy, but I couldn't help it. Usually, it was tough for me to make close friends so quickly. But these three already knew the real me.

I made a silent vow to do whatever it took to help us win — even if it meant squashing my inner wallflower. After all, it was the least a secret weapon could do!

Chapter 2

When we entered the gym, we found total madness. The volleyball team was using half of the floor for their practice, and our squad had totally taken over the rest of it. Coach Adkins was stationed in the corner passing out cheer camp outfits (it's a tradition for teams to match every day).

"I feel bad for whoever has to stand next to me in formation," said Ella Jenkins. Of course Ella would *have* to rush to the locker room and try on her outfits as soon as she got them. She was clearly proud of how her long legs looked in the hot pink shorts that read "CHEER" across the back.

"I look *fiiiine*," she added. Coming from anyone else, I would have thought they were joking, but Ella? Not so much. She was a bit . . . well . . . full of herself.

"Yeah, smokin' is more like it!" said Kacey Kosir, modeling her own tank top and shorts ensemble. Kacey was Ella's faithful sidekick.

Ella noticed me standing there. "Oh, hey, Faith, you still need to get yours," she said, grabbing my hand and leading me toward boxes with sizes marked on them. She pointed to the box marked L. "I'm guessing you ordered a large."

Kacey stifled a giggle, and I just looked down. It was no secret that I was the tallest girl on the team, but I couldn't believe how rude she was. Luckily, Lissa overheard and stepped in.

"Well, we all know what the L stands for when *you're* involved," Lissa told Ella, making the "loser" sign with her fingers. She had no patience for snobs. "C'mon, Faith, Coach A's got your packet over here."

I shot Lissa a grateful look and followed her over to Coach Adkins. "Higgins, here's yours," Coach barked, handing me several plastic bags with clothing items inside. Sometimes I wondered if she even knew our first names!

Lissa grabbed hers, too, and after sticking them in our cheer duffels, we sat down with the others for our team meeting. Always the prepared one, Brooke was going over her packing list for camp and getting suggestions from the other girls. "Should I bring a few *Teen Vogues*, or do you think we'll be too busy to read?" she wondered aloud.

"I'm pretty sure we'll be too busy to sleep!" said Gaby. "Seems like they pack something into every single minute."

"Yeah, you're probably right," said Brooke, crossing the magazines off her list. "But maybe I'll pack my new **Zoey Dean*** book just in case. And what about last year's spirit stick? Should I bring it for good luck?"

―――――――

*All my friends love Zoey Dean and her A-List books! When it comes to fun books, there's nothing like reading about the crazy lives of superrich teens.

Packing checklist

√ Alarm clock

√ Bedding

√ Camera

√ Ponytail holders, headbands,
  and ribbons

√ Water bottle

_ Healthy snacks

_ Practice outfits and uniform

_ Sunscreen

_ Any medication you normally take

_ Props: think poms, signs, megaphones

√ A great attitude that is ready for fun!

Before I could ask her what a spirit stick was, Coach Adkins blew her whistle to get our attention. "Girls, we've got a lot to do today, so settle down and listen up," she commanded. I made a mental note to ask Gaby if Coach had ever been in the military. She was always so gruff!

"Okay, first things first. Let's review our clothes. Who wants to tell me what we're wearing on Day One?" Coach asked. Trina Mathews's hand shot up.

"We'll be sporting this lovely green tank top and gold shorts," she said, springing up to twirl around like a model while holding up the clothes. Not surprising — she was a total fashionista. The outfit was cute: the tank top featured a cursive G on the front for Greenview, and the shorts were gold with green polka dots.

"Thank you, Heidi Klum," joked Coach. "What about Day Two?"

Mackenzie Potz volunteered, showing off our "CHEER" shorts along with a fitted, black half-top.

"And you better all know what to bring for Day Three," said Coach. Everyone's heads nodded solemnly. Day Three was the big camp competition, and we'd be wearing our basketball uniforms. Sleeveless and sleek, they were better suited for the warm summer temps than our bulky uniforms for football season. "Make sure your uniforms are crisp, pressed, and ready to go. And don't forget your shoes!"

She went over a few other reminders, like making sure to get enough sleep the night before and bringing healthy snacks and water bottles. It was definitely a lot to remember! As I was trying to process it all in my head, Coach A called my name and snapped me out of it.

"Higgins, your mom is driving one of the carpool teams, correct?" she asked.

"Yes, Coach, she'll be driving Gaby, Lissa, and Brooke, and me," I said. Gaby caught my eye and made a funny face, and I had a feeling the two-hour drive would be a fun one. Coach checked something off on her list and gave me an approving glance before moving on to confirm the other carpool teams.

Brooke, Lissa, and Gaby tipped their heads together and started whispering. I couldn't help but wonder how such opposites had become so tight. There was Brooke: confident, supersmart, and a bit of an overachiever. (Okay, a major over-achiever.) Then there was Gaby: flirty, fun, and well, slightly spacey. And, of course, Miss Lissa: ultrasassy, full of fire, and fiercely loyal.

So where did I fit into all of this? I wasn't sure. I'm pretty quiet, but I've also got a decent sense of humor once people know me. And I'm always there to listen when my friends need to vent. Personally, I thought the four of us made a good team — I just hoped they agreed! Having built-in friends when school started would save me from weeks of lunches by myself.

Everyone stood up. It was time to run through our competition routine. Brooke turned to me and raised her hand for a high-five. "You ready to rock this, Higgins?" she joked, imitating Coach A.

I high-fived her right back. "So ready we need a new word for ready," I said, and did a round-off to illustrate my point. And I was. As far as I was concerned, camp was just the beginning of a whole new start for me. And I could barely wait!

chapter 3

As I stared out the window of my mom's car, it was clear we were far from the Greenview city limits. Rows of crops filled fields as far as the eye could see, and houses were few and far between. I could see cows and horses grazing, looking lazy and relaxed.

"Looks like we're not in Kansas anymore, Toto! Oh wait, maybe we are in Kansas," I quipped, getting a laugh from Gaby, Faith, and Brooke.

"Very funny, Faith," said my mom, patting my leg from the driver's seat. "If it weren't for these farms, you wouldn't have all those tasty organic vegetables that I use for our meals." My mom was kind of a hippie and loved to buy everything local. She ran an eco-friendly interior design business, so she was all tree-hugger and stuff.

"There's no good radio stations anymore," complained Gaby. "Faith, can we turn on that mix I made? I need to hear a little Shakira."

"Sure, but I think we're almost there," I told her, putting the CD in the player. "The last sign said Rosen College is just ten miles away."

"Yeah, I recognize some of this stuff from last year," said Brooke, peering out the window. "I can't imagine going to college out here in the boonies!"

Rosen College Road Trip Mix!
1. Hips Don't Lie, Shakira
2. Let's Get Loud, JLo
3. Just Dance, Lady Gaga
4. What Is Love? Hadaway
5. I Gotta Feeling, Black Eyed Peas
6. Down, Jay Sean
7. Stronger, Kenye West
8. Hey Ya! Outkast
9. Hollaback Girl, Gwen Stefani
10. So What, Pink

My most favorite song ever!

"That's because you already know you're going to Stanford," teased Lissa. We were only in eighth grade, but Brooke's dad had his heart set on her following his footsteps and attending his old school. If Brooke had her way, she'd probably rather take a cheer scholarship to a Big 10 school. Luckily, they had four more years to figure it out!

"Whatever, Marks," said Brooke, and she and Lissa started play-fighting in the backseat. My mom just gave me a little smile. Normally she probably would have been annoyed, but I think she was just happy that I was fitting in okay.

THE BIG 10 (otherwise known as amazing schools to cheer for!)

- University of Illinois at Urbana–Champaign
- Indiana University
- University of Iowa
- University of Michigan
- Michigan State University
- University of Minnesota
- University of Nebraska–Lincoln
- Northwestern University
- Ohio State University
- Pennsylvania State University
- Purdue University
- University of Wisconsin–Madison

My #1 choice right now!

A few dance songs later, we were pulling into the long winding drive of Rosen College's entryway.

It was the **Universal Cheerleaders Association*** camp location nearest to Greenview, and our squad attended camp here every year. As we pulled past the main quad, all I could see was a sea of cheerleaders!

"I think we're supposed to check into our rooms first and then meet everyone on the quad," Brooke said, looking at the schedule Coach Adkins had passed out.

Using the campus map, my mom found the dorm building that would be our home the next few nights. A few buff college guys helped us get our things up to our room, and we ran into Ella, Kacey, and Trina on the way.

"I see you girls made it all right," said Ella. "We thought maybe you got lost in the cornfields!"

~~~~~~~

*The universal Cheerleaders Association is one of the leading cheer organizations in the country. They host camps and sponsor competitions. Like our squad, they believe that cheerleaders' main job is to support the athletes and lead the crowds!

Kacey and Trina giggled obediently.

"See you out there," called Kacey as the trio flounced off.

"Could she be any more annoying?" I asked. For some reason, Ella had a way of getting under my skin.

"Don't sweat it," said Gaby, putting her arm around me. "We'll freeze her bra later or something old-school like that."

My mom poked her head out of our room down the hallway. "I've got your bed all ready!" she called. "Gaby, do you want me to make yours?"

"Um . . . yeah!" said Gaby. Turning to me, she added, "Your mom totally rocks."

Once we got to our room, we noticed that Coach A had hung little megaphone signs on the door with our names on them. *Cute!* I guess even Coach A had her friendly moments.

We managed to settle in pretty quickly, and Gaby and I both changed into our green and gold outfits for the day. I glanced at my watch and realized it was almost noon. Time to get down to the quad!

My mom followed my stare. "I guess I should get going so you girls can have your fun," she said, unsuccessfully trying not to sound sad.

I gulped. I'd never spent a night this far away from home before. I didn't think it would be a big deal, but suddenly, I felt scared and overwhelmed.

"Yeah, I guess so," I muttered.

Gaby must have sensed what was going on, because she leapt up from the bed. "I'll let you two say your goodbyes in private," she said, giving my mom a quick hug. "Thanks for the ride, Mrs. H. Are you going to come to the awards ceremony in a few days?"

"I'll be there with bells on," said my mom, pulling me close.

"Okay, great! Faith, I'll see you down there," said Gaby, skipping out the door.

I looked up at my mom with sad eyes. "Well, I guess it's only a few days, right?" I asked, searching for reassurance.

"Absolutely, and I know you're in good hands with Coach Adkins and Gaby and the girls," said my mom. "And you know we're just a phone call away."

"If they even get reception out here in No Man's Land," I said, trying to lighten the mood.

"You'll find a way if you need us," said my mom. "Just think, a few months ago, you weren't even a cheerleader yet. This is a big deal! I want you to enjoy every minute of this experience. Promise?" She held out her hand for a pinky swear.

I linked my pinky with hers and shook. "Promise."

chapter 4

By the time I made it down to the quad, all the other Greenview girls were already there. (Apparently, I was the only crybaby of the bunch.) Sheena Hays, another teammate, greeted me with excitement. "Hey, Faith!" she called. "The staff show is about to start."

As if on cue, loud music filled the air, and everyone started screaming. The energy in the room was incredible! "Cheerleaders, are you READY?" screamed the MC over the noise. The sound rose to a deafening roar. "Presenting this year's UCA Camp staff!"

Up in front, cheerleaders sporting UCA uniforms started tumbling and doing difficult college-level partner stunts. One guy even held up two girls in a **double cupie***! Everyone whooped and started clapping to the beat. The energy was totally amped up. For a moment, I got lost in what was happening and forgot about feeling homesick.

As the MC introduced each staffer over the mic, each guy or girl did an insanely high jump or some sort of amazing trick, like a **standing back tuck****. It was kind of cool to learn which colleges they all cheered for. The staff came from all over and traveled together from camp to camp. It would be a really cool job, but I couldn't imagine how terrifying it would be to have a whole camp's worth of cheerleaders' eyes on me. I could never do it!

* The first time I saw a double cupie in real life, I just about flipped! It was so cool. One guy holding two girls straight above his head. Fabulous. If you've never seen it, you should Google it!

** A standing back tuck is crazy. The cheerleader does a back flip from a standing position. I cannot imagine nailing something like that!

As the show died down, one of the guy cheerleaders stepped forward and took the mic from the MC. "I said A-BOOM-CHICKA-BOOM!" he yelled.

"I SAID A-BOOM-CHICKA-BOOM!" the whole camp repeated. I shot Gaby a confused look, but she was yelling right back with everyone else.

"I SAID A-BOOM-CHICKA-ROCKA-CHICKA-ROCKA-CHICKA-BOOM!" he yelled, and everyone repeated him again. I decided to just go with the flow and yell along.

"UH-HUH!"
"UH-HUH!"
"OH YEAH!"
"OH YEAH!"

"ONE MORE TIME?"
"ONE MORE TIME!"
"SOUTHERN STYLE!"
"SOUTHERN STYLE!"

Huh? Southern style? I had no idea what they were talking about. But then the leaders repeated the cheer again, except this time in Southern accents. Then we did it again in Valley Girl style. It was all confusing and a little overwhelming for me. But for everyone else it was clearly a beloved camp tradition. Once the cheer was over, everyone erupted into mad applause again. Coach A just stood over to the side, shaking her head and grinning.

"You know what time it is?" yelled the guy again.

"IT'S PEANUT BUTTER AND JELLY TIME!"

everyone yelled back, and then a rap song about PB&J came over the loudspeaker. All the cheerleaders went crazy dancing around, including our team. I just hoped I would get the hang of all these inside jokes at some point! I was having fun, but I felt a little lost.

Once everybody settled down a little, another staffer gave a speech about how the next few days would play out. There would be lots of classes where we'd learn dances and cheers to

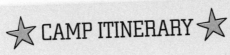

⭐ CAMP ITINERARY ⭐

DAY 1		DAY 2		DAY 3	
10:30	Check in	7:00	Breakfast	7:00	Breakfast
12:15	Welcome	8:00	Rise-and-shine stretch session	8:00	Rise-and-shine stretch session
1:00	Dance class	8:20	Elective sessions: Stunting, tumbling, or fight-song choreography; Snack break at 10:00	8:20	Review and practice. Meet with your team and big bro or sis. Review all you've learned at camp, and practice your Camp Champ routines.
2:30	Snack				
2:45	Cheer/Chant class				
4:15	Ice breakers. Meet your fellow campers	11:30	Lunch break	11:30	Lunch break
		12:30	Jump class	12:30	Camp Champ competition
5:00	Dinner break	1:30	Dance class		
6:00	Evaluation practice	3:00	Snack	3:00	Awards and camp farewell
7:00	Evaluation #1	3:15	Cheer class		
7:45	Review & awards	4:15	Team practice session		
8:45	Break for the night	5:15	Evaluation #2		
		6:00	Dinner break		
10:00	Lights out	7:00	Individual jump contest		
		7:45	Dance party!		
		9:00	Break for the night		
		10:00	Lights out		

take back and perform in our hometowns. We'd also take part in stunting seminars. Evaluations and competitions would be held at the end of each day to see how well we were absorbing the material. Oh, and there would be fun stuff sprinkled in there too, like a dance party and other activities.

"Before we break off into groups, we want each team to meet their big bro or big sis!" yelled one of the leaders. "They'll be helping you throughout camp and are here to help each squad reach their highest potential! So give 'em a big hand!" He motioned to the staffers standing behind him, and everyone cheered again.

He started yelling off names. "Greenview Middle, your big sis is Charlene from North Carolina State University!" A tiny, yet muscular, blonde broke out from the pack, wiggling **spirit fingers*** and running toward us.

---

* Spirit fingers is one of those goofy cheer/dance terms you hear all the time. You just hold out your hands and move your fingers back and forth. If it's done right, it seems like you're watching energy!

"Hey, y'all," she drawled sweetly as she approached. "I'm Charlene! We're going to have a great time the next few days." All the girls introduced themselves excitedly.

It was time for dance class. Charlene sat down with us as some of the other staffers showed us the routine. Soon we were up on our feet, learning each **8-count*** one by one.

Even though the temperature was rising, the staffers' energy was contagious and kept us moving. It was cool having Charlene dance with us, too. It was way easier to copy the movements by seeing them up close.

"Let's try it with the music," yelled the leader, and a hip-hop mash-up started playing. Ella pushed her way to the front and started doing over-the-top **facials**** as she danced.

* An 8-count is a section of dance. Each count matches a beat in the music. Breaking a routine up this way makes it easier to learn.

** Facials are big expressions that make you look like you're having a blast, even if you are super nervous. Huge smiles, a wink here and there, maybe a head bob . . . they are all part of it. It sounds weird, but judges like to see those big grins during competition.

I saw Brooke and Gaby glance at each other and roll their eyes. "Looks like somebody's campaigning for All-Star already," grumbled Lissa after we finished running through the counts.

"What's All-Star?" I asked.

Charlene overheard me and walked over. "All-Stars are chosen by the staff and get to perform at the **Macy's Thanksgiving Day parade*** in New York," she told me. "Tomorrow night during camp evals, we'll have a tryout for anyone who wants to be one. You should go for it!"

"Yeah, Faith, show 'em your stuff!" said Gaby. "I know I'm gonna try out."

"No thanks," I said, shaking my head. "I'm still adjusting to performing with a group, let alone by myself! I don't really like being the center of attention."

---

* Hey, the Macy's Thanksgiving Day parade is actually on my bucket list! Obviously I don't want to perform in the parade. (The TV audience, plus the people watching on the street, would make me so nervous!) But I would totally love to help walk one of those HUGE balloons down the street. How fun!

"Um, then why did you try out for cheerleading?" asked Ella from up front. She'd clearly been listening in since Charlene joined the conversation. "That's kind of what it's all about. Or did you think you'd signed up for the Mathletes?" As always, Kacey giggled on cue. I felt my face blazing.

The music started up again, so I didn't have to think of a comeback, thankfully. "I think you'd rock it, Faith," whispered Charlene. "Don't let her get to you!"

Easier said than done, but luckily, it was hard to stay down for long among hundreds of upbeat cheerleaders. The positive vibes were definitely a-flowing! I managed to regain my composure and nailed down the routine by the end of class.

"Whoo! Is it nap time yet?" I joked to Brooke as we took a Gatorade break. The hot sun was relentless.

"Girl, this is just the beginning!" she said dramatically. "Camp is like a marathon — it's go, go, go from the second you get here."

"Well, in that case, goooooo Greenview!" I joked, hitting a number-one move. "Can't wait to see what the rest of the day has in store."

And as Brooke, Lissa, Gaby, and I clinked our cups in solidarity, I forgot all about Ella.

SQUAD!
CHEER!
CHEER!
Yell!
FLY!
CHANT!
CHEER!
!
Cheer
CHOP!
SQUAD!
¡SPIRIS!
CHANT!
ip
OH
FLY!
SPIRIT!
Cheer.
CHEER
eer!
CHANT!
YELL!
CHEER!
FLY!
Cheer!
Yell!
¡Jump!
¡CHEER!
SPIRIT!
SQUAD!
SPIRIT!
Cheer!
CHEE
Jump!
SPIRIT!
SPIRIT!
CHEER!
Cheer!
Squad!
dump!
FLY!
SQUAD!
SPIRIT!
Ch
Cheer!
YELL!
Cheer.
SPIRIT!
Cheer!
Yell!
CHEER!
CHANT!
CHEER
Cheer!
CHEER!
CHEER!
FLY!
CHEER!
CHANT!
FLY!
SPIRIT
CHEER!
Cheer!
CHANT!
CHEER!
SQUAD!
SPIRIT
CHANT!
FLY!
CHEER!
CHEER!
Cheer!
¡CHANT!
FL
YELL!
Cheer
Jump

Chapter 5

Four hours later, my head was spinning. Brooke wasn't kidding about camp being a marathon! Along with the dance routine, we'd learned three new sideline chants and a floor cheer, plus met dozens of cheerleaders from squads all over the state.

Now we were leaving dinner at Nelson Dining Hall to head over to the quad again and practice for our first eval.

"I'm not sure what's worse — the mystery meat back at Greenview or the food here," said Gaby. She thought about food more than anyone I know. "Is this what we have to look forward to in college?"

"Probably," said Brooke. "But the freedom will be worth it!" Gaby didn't look so sure.

"Hey, who's in our eval group tonight?" asked Lissa. For the evals, they split the cheer teams up into groups of four in order to save time.

"We're with Pioneer Middle, Dante Heights, and Howell City Junior High," I answered.

"Ooh, that'll give us a chance to see if Pioneer is any good this year," said Lissa, rubbing her hands together. She was extra competitive. "Hey, there's Charlene over there!"

Charlene was under some trees, working with Kacey on her tumbling. Our teammate Britt Bolton was standing by, cheering her on. Some of the other Greenview girls were working on a formation for the eval routine. I couldn't believe how much energy everyone still had!

"Okay, everybody," said Charlene once we were all ready to practice. "Who's got some ideas for the eval routine? It needs to include one cheer and one sideline chant."

Ella's hand shot up. "What if we start with the 'Yell out' sideline, and then do the cheer? It could even finish with a group stunt."

Everyone seemed cool with that, including Coach A, so we went to work putting it all together. The end result had us starting off standing in a **V formation***, and then the girls in back would tumble forward so that we were all in a straight line for the cheer. It was a really cool idea! To finish things off, we'd transition into two stunt groups that would do **side-by-side elevators****.

"Let's run through the whole thing," instructed Coach Adkins after we'd put all the pieces together. We hit our starting places, and Brooke called the chant: **"READY?"**

"SET!" we answered as a group.

⁓⁓⁓⁓

* To picture a V formation, think of how geese fly and you pretty much have it. One person stands in front with pairs of cheerleaders standing behind, forming a V shape.

** In an elevator, the flyer jumps into the hands of the bases and is lifted to shoulder level. The bases all face inward toward each other.

YELL OUT YOUR COLORS,
GREENVIEW BLUE
AND RED!

The chant repeated four times, with the tumbling formation transition during the final part. We all hit a **high V*** with our arms while we dropped to our knees as the ending pose. Then it was time for the cheer:

STEP IT UP, VIKING FANS
GET ON YOUR FEET AND CHEER
YELL FOR THE VIKES
'CUZ THIS IS OUR YEAR!

On the word "year," our stunt groups raised Brooke and Gaby into elevator extensions, and they hit **touchdown**** motions on top of the stunt. It was a pretty solid finish! All of a sudden, we heard clapping from across the way.

---

* To make a high V, raise your arms up and make a V shape above your head, with the fists facing outward. No broken wrists!

** A touchdown is another arm position. Hold both arms directly over your head, straight and tight against the head. Your hands should be in fists with the palms facing each other.

"Awesome job!" yelled one of the Dante Heights girls.

"Work it, girls," called another.

Mackenzie started clapping and yelled, "HEY DANTE HEIGHTS, WE'VE GOT SPIRIT, YES WE DO, WE'VE GOT SPIRIT, HOW 'BOUT YOU?"

The Dante Heights girls were quick to yell back, "YES, YES, YES, WE DO, WE'VE GOT SPIRIT, HOW 'BOUT YOU?"

It went back and forth a few times before everyone started screaming and jumping around. Charlene smiled approvingly. "Keep that up, ladies, and you'll be sure to get a spirit stick later!" Apparently, the squads with the best sportsmanship and spirit got awarded a spirit stick — so that's how it worked.

We practiced a few more times after that, and then it was time for the eval. Several of the camp staffers acted as judges, and each squad took the grass to perform their version of what we'd learned that day. It was cool to see all the creative interpretations the teams had!

CAMP EVALUATION

DATE: SQUAD:

OVERALL PERFORMANCE		CHEERS/STUNTS	
1. Entrance	4 3 2 1	1. Sharp motions	4 3 2 1
2. Spirit	4 3 2 1	2. Climbing technique	4 3 2 1
3. Use of signs	4 3 2 1	3. Timing	4 3 2 1
4. Jumps	4 3 2 1	4. Formation	4 3 2 1
5. Tumbling	4 3 2 1	5. Knowledge of material	4 3 2 1
6. Smiles	4 3 2 1	6. Perfection of stunts	4 3 2 1
7. Voices	4 3 2 1		
8. Dancing	4 3 2 1		

Performance section total: ___

Cheers/stunts section total: ___

Final total: _____

Comments:

RATING CHART

50-56 points: Superior
36-49 points: Excellent
28-35 points: Outstanding
14-27 points: Good

After we'd all performed (and Pioneer *was* awesome), the judges took a few minutes to talk, and then they had us all sit down on the grass. "You guys did an awesome job today," said Troy, who was a cheerleader at Ohio State University. "So who's ready for the results?" Everyone wooed and screamed in response.

"Okay, Dante Heights, you get . . . an Outstanding ribbon!" called Lauren, a University of Kentucky cheerleader. She ran over to give the Dante girls their ribbon, and everybody clapped in support.

"And Howell City High, you get . . . an Excellent ribbon!" called Troy, and several of the Howell City girls ran up excitedly to grab it from him.

"Give it up for Pioneer Middle, because they get . . . a Superior ribbon!" said Mark, who cheered for Louisiana State. The Pioneer girls started screaming and high-fiving. Brooke and Lissa exchanged a look. Gaby grabbed my hand in anticipation of what our ribbon would be.

"And last, but not least, Greenview Middle, you get . . . an Excellent ribbon!" called Charlene with a big smile. She ran over to award it to us, and gave us a big group hug.

Everyone clapped, but some of the Greenview girls didn't seem as jazzed as before. Before I could debrief the results, Troy took the mic again. "Way to go, guys! Seriously, awesome job, everyone," he said. "Now it's time to head over to the fieldhouse for review and more awards — see you there!"

Gaby pulled an Evian spray out of her bag and started misting herself with it. "I can't take this heat anymore," she complained. "I'm starting to feel like a fried egg!"

"Well, there's AC in the field house, thankfully," said Brooke, pulling Gaby up from the ground. "Let's hope we at least get a spirit stick to make up for the Excellent ribbon. I totally thought we had Superior in the bag."

"Yeah, we'll have to bring our A-game tomorrow, or we'll have no shot at Camp Champs," grumbled Lissa.

It was all starting to make sense. "So Superior is better than Excellent, right?" I asked. "What about Outstanding?"

Ella jumped in. "It means, 'Thanks for playing, but you're not really a contender,'" she said. "I would die if we got that."

Coach Adkins overheard and quickly corrected her. "Ella, it simply means that the squad has room for improvement," she said. "We've got plenty of work to do ourselves, ladies. Now get to it! The review starts in five minutes."

And we all skipped down to the fieldhouse, singing the "Boom-Chicka-Boom" song the whole way.

CHEER!
Yell!
FLY!
CHEER!
Cheer!
CHANT!
Yell!
SPIRIT!
CHEER!
Cheer!
YELL!
Cheer!
Cheer!
CHANT!
FLY!
CHEER!
CHANT!
Cheer!
CHEER!
SQUAD!
FLY!
Cheer!
CHANT!
YELL!

chapter 6

After a solid day of dancing, stunting, and chanting,
I found myself with some alone time back in the room.
Gaby had made friends with some Dante Heights girls and
was visiting them on the floor below us. She was the queen
of instant popularity!

Cheer camp was a blast, but it was also exhausting! So
it was really good to have some time to myself. When I sat
down on my bed, I instantly crashed. I started to lie down,
but felt something crinkly as my hand slid under my pillow.
It turned out to be a note left by my mom!

Thinking of you, Faith. We love you and are so proud of you, honey! Knock 'em dead. Cheers, Mom

Tears welled up in my eyes all over again. It felt like years instead of hours since she'd dropped me off. I wasn't sure if I was just overtired or truly homesick, but suddenly I wanted nothing more than to be home in my own bed. I started to wonder if Coach Adkins might let me borrow her cell to call my mom, but before I could go find out, Gaby breezed into the room.

"Hey Faith-a-roo!" she exclaimed, totally oblivious to my crying spell. "Those girls from Dante are such a hoot." Gaby was untying her green hair bow when she noticed my expression in the mirror. She scurried over to sit with me on the bed.

"What's wrong, girl? There's no crying at cheer camp!" she joked, making a reference to one of our fave flicks, *A League of Their Own**.

"Oh, not much," I said, wiping my eyes. I didn't want to be a baby, so I was trying to play it down. "My mom wrote me a sappy note, and I got a little emotional. It's no big deal."

"Aww, look at Mrs. H being all sweet!" Gaby put her arm around me. "Don't worry, Faith. The sleepover craziness starts soon, and you'll forget you ever shed a tear."

"Huh?" I asked. "Isn't it almost lights out?" The leaders had given us a strict speech about getting enough sleep and obeying the camp curfew.

"Oh, nobody follows that," said Gaby, giggling. "Everyone knows the real reason you come to camp is for the bonding. We always meet up in Brooke's room and continue the fun on the DL. Even Ella joins in — miracle of miracles."

---

* A League of Their Own is the ultimate chick flick. It is based on the true-life story of a female professional baseball team. The line "There's no crying in baseball" is one of the most famous movie quotes of all time.

"I had no idea!" I exclaimed. "Is Coach A down with this undercover stuff?"

"I'm pretty sure she knows, but she turns a blind eye," said Gaby. "All the squad coaches do."

Just then, Maddie Todd and Kate Ellis poked their heads into the room. "Hey slowpokes, you coming to Brooke and Lissa's or what? Everyone's already in there."

Gaby and I locked eyes, and hers searched mine to see if I was okay. I nodded and grabbed her hand. "You know it! Let's go."

When we walked in, our whole squad was crammed into the tiny room. Everyone was wearing PJs, and some of the girls even had curlers and facial masks on. Taking it all in, it totally looked like a sleepover straight out of the movies! All we needed was a Sandra Dee clone, and it'd be *Grease** all over again.

━━∿∿∿∿∿∿━━

* Grease is one of those movies that your grandparents loved, then your parents loved, and now you should love. A musical love story set in the 1950s, it doesn't get much more fun than watching John Travolta dance away with Olivia Newton-John.

And it seemed like spirits had definitely lifted since we'd been awarded a spirit stick during the evening's award ceremony.

"Okay, girlies, there's just one rule. We have to try to stay quiet," ordered Brooke, using the spirit stick as a fake microphone. "If I get in trouble with Coach A, there go my chances of making captain."

"Yes, sir!" said Mackenzie, and she and Sheena dissolved into giggles. Brooke couldn't help but laugh, too.

"So who does everyone think is the cutest guy cheerleader on staff?" Trina asked, sitting cross-legged on Lissa's bed.

"Oh, that's easy," answered Gaby, who was braiding Maddie's long red hair. "Troy by far! He is gorgeous!"

Kacey busted out her cam, and we all started looking at videos she'd taken throughout the day, pointing out guys we thought were cute. They were all so adorable!

"I have an idea," said Ella. "Let's play Truth or Dare!"
I braced myself, trying to stay invisible.

"This could be dangerous," said Brooke, giggling. "Last year, you tried to get me to sneak into the wrestling dorm!"

"Oh, like you didn't want to," joked Lissa. "You're lucky the guard wouldn't let you leave!"

~~~~~~~~~~ TRUTH OR DARE ~~~~~~~~

IDEAS FOR DARE

* Lick the floor.
* Sing "I'm a Little Teapot," and be sure to use the actions.
* Do your best Michael Jackson impression.
* Lick the bottom of your own foot.
* Dance with a mop or broom.
* Sing your favorite show tune for at least one minute.
* Choose your favorite animal, then imitate it for thirty seconds.
* Put a piece of ice down your shirt and dance until it falls out.
* Try to put your feet behind your head.
* Let the person on your right do your makeup—blindfolded.

TRUTH OR DARE

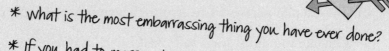

IDEAS FOR TRUTH

* What is the most embarrassing thing you have ever done?
* If you had to marry a boy in our class, who would you pick?
* Have you had your first kiss?
* What is your favorite thing about the person on your left?
* Who has the best hair in the room?
* If you could read minds, whose mind would you read first?
* Have you ever peed in a pool?
* What five words would you use to describe yourself?
* When is the last time you cried and why?
* If the school paper did an article about you, what would you want them to write?

"Yeah, let's play," said Mackenzie, and some of the other girls murmured their agreement. "I'll go first. Gaby, truth or dare?"

"Um, dare," said Gaby, scrunching her face in anticipation.

"Okay, I dare you to . . . wrap yourself up like a mummy in toilet paper and do a lap around this floor," said Mackenzie, giggling.

"No way!" said Gaby, but she was giggling, too. Lissa and Kate ran to the bathroom. They came back with a few rolls of TP.

They got to work dressing Gaby up, and soon she was ready for her mission. Sheena and Mackenzie volunteered to follow her down the hall to make sure she did it!

Everyone started laughing uncontrollably as Gaby stumbled into the hallway, grunting and making zombie sounds. A few minutes later, they returned, out of breath from laughing so hard. "You should have seen it!" said Sheena. "The Pioneer Middle girls were totally weirded out!"

Gaby busted free from her toilet paper costume, a huge, triumphant grin on her face. "Okay, my turn," she said, plopping down on Brooke's bed. "Ella, truth . . . or dare?"

"Truth," said Ella, rolling her eyes. I was surprised she could even be bothered to play "little kid" games, since she considered herself so sophisticated.

"Okay, if you had to cast me, Brooke, and Lissa in a movie, which actresses would play us?" asked Gaby.

"Oooh, good one," said Ella, deep in thought. "Well, Lissa's easy — I would totally cast Selena Gomez. For Brooke, probably Dakota Fanning? And for you, Gabs, I think Ashley Tisdale."

Gaby stood up dramatically. "I like the sound of that!" she exclaimed. "Hollywood, I'm ready for my close-up." She pretended to faint, and Brooke and Lissa caught her. Everyone giggled again.

"All right, it's my turn now," said Ella, scanning the room with her eyes. Unfortunately, they landed on me. "Faith, step up to the plate. I've got a good one for you." Everyone ooh-ed, waiting to hear what she was going to say. Meanwhile I was terrified.

Ella lowered her voice dramatically. "I want you to go knock on Coach A's door and run back here before she catches you!"

I froze. "Um, don't I have a choice between truth and dare?"

"Well, if you're *scared*, don't bother playing at all," said Ella, crossing her arms indignantly.

"Yeah, c'mon, Faith, it'll be legendary if you get away with it," said Kate.

"Faith! Faith! Faith! Faith! Faith!" everyone started chanting, before Brooke shushed them furiously. She didn't want us to get caught.

"Sorry to disappoint, guys, but there's no way I could pull that off," I said, feeling pretty lame. "Plus, if Coach A finds out we're all in here, the party's over, period."

"Fine, you get a pass this time," said Ella. "But before camp ends, you *will* do some sort of dare. It's only fair."

I didn't *dare* let myself think about what that would be.

chapter 7

"Faith, what's up, *chiquita?**" whispered Lissa the next morning as she arched her back in a cat stretch. "You've been mute all morning."

It was the rise-and-shine stretch session, and squads were sprawled out all over the lawn getting limber for the day ahead. A chill song was playing, and the mood was rather low-key. Well, as low-key as three hundred cheerleaders can be, I guess!

***

* chiquita = girlfriend, as in "Chiquita, you can trust me, so tell me what's up!"

A stretch session was just what I needed. I hadn't gotten much sleep the night before. I'd tossed and turned, wishing I was home and worrying about what dare Ella would come up with for me.

"Nothing major," I said, playing it down. I didn't want anyone listening to know how much Ella had gotten to me. Plus, I was kind of afraid the other girls thought I was a chicken after the way I'd handled the dare. I just didn't really feel like talking to anyone. "I guess I'm still just waking up."

Lissa looked at me with confusion. She knew I was a total morning person. At home, I usually got up early to paint on my bedroom balcony, read, or just relax in my mom's garden. But Lissa didn't press the issue.

Pretty soon, Troy took the mic to explain the morning agenda. "Okay, here's how the morning is going to go down," he told us. "Next up are the elective sessions, where you'll have the choice of stunting class, tumbling class, or learning a new fight song. Stunt class will be down by the lake, tumblers will be in the field house, and the fight song will be taught here on the quad. Discuss amongst yourselves!"

An upbeat hip-hop song came over the loudspeaker as cheerleaders started to stand up and get energized. Coach Adkins called us all together for a powwow.

"I think it makes the most sense if we send four girls to each class," she said, doing a quick head count to make sure we were all there. "That way, when we get back to Greenview, we can all teach each other what we learned."

That seemed like a good strategy, so we decided our resident gymnasts Lissa, Kate, Maddie, and Britt would hit the tumbling class, while Ella, Kacey, Trina, and Gaby would go learn the fight song choreography. That left me, Mackenzie, Brooke, and Sheena to attend stunt class.

I was down with that plan, especially since it kept me out of Ella's orbit for the morning. I was pretty stressed about whether she'd make good on her promise, so the more time I could buy, the better!

Charlene, Mark, and a few of the other staffers were leading the stunt class. I wondered what it would be like to stunt on grass instead of on mats like in the gym back home. At least there was a nice breeze coming off the lake.

"So you've been watching us do lots of cool partner stunts and group lifts," said Mark, as Charlene and a guy cheerleader loaded into a **liberty heel stretch***. "Now it's your turn. Today we're going to show you some multibase stunts that you can perform all year long. First up? **Liberty extensions****!**"

Everyone clapped, and I felt my mood lift a little. I was a base in our stunt group, and stunting was still so fun and new to me. Most people wanted to be flyers, but I was totally fine with being a behind-the-scenes base.

~~~~~~~~

* When Charlene did the liberty heel stretch with her partner, it was just the two of them. At our age level, two or three bases would hold on to one foot of the flyer. She would then extend her other leg and hold that other foot in a stretched-out position near her head.

** The heel stretch was a bit advanced to start out with, so we were starting with liberty extensions (or libs). Again, the bases hold the foot of the flyer, while her opposite leg is bent with the foot next to the standing leg's knee.

70

(Plus, I'm so tall I probably couldn't be a flyer even if I wanted!)

I'd been learning things here and there at our summer practices. But it was awesome to have actual class focused on stunting.

We watched Charlene and the guys demonstrate once. Then we broke into groups to learn step by step. Charlene came over to help us. "Okay, so who's the flyer here?" she asked, and Brooke raised her hand.

"Perfect," said Charlene, taking Mackenzie by the shoulders to move her over to face Sheena. "Okay, you two are about the same height, so you'll be the side bases. Faith, can you be the back spot?" I nodded and took my place between them.

The steps were pretty straightforward. Brooke was supposed to stand in the center and place her right foot in Mackenzie's and Sheena's hands as they crouched. I'd plant my hand on her bottom and help hoist her high into the air.

Once Brooke was up, our arms would straighten and she'd balance one foot in our hands. The other leg would be bent with foot to knee.

"Let's practice just the loading-in part a few times," instructed Charlene. "Don't lift Brooke all the way yet."

We did the prep a few times with flying colors, no pun intended! Charlene gave us the go-ahead to try the whole thing. "Remember, clap on two, crouch on three, **load in*** on five, lift on six!"

And with that, we tried the whole stunt for the first time. Charlene counted aloud to guide us through it. But as we started to lift Brooke, she lost her footing and fell forward. "You okay?" I asked, worried.

"Totally fine," she reassured me, straightening up and shaking it off. "Don't worry. It comes with the flyer territory! I've got this."

~~~~~~~~

* During load in, the flyer steps into position on the bases and gets ready for the lift. It's a good time to be focused.

We decided to go for it again, and on the second try, we got Brooke all the way up. She was a bit wobbly at first, but managed to steady herself and regain balance. Several of the other groups stopped to watch us and started clapping. Once Brooke had been up for several seconds, Charlene yelled the cue to cradle down, and we caught her in the dismount.

"Now that's what I call a lib!" said Charlene, clapping in appreciation. "You guys really caught on quick."

"Wow, maybe we can even put it in our Camp Champs routine," said Mackenzie, and Brooke widened her eyes in excitement.

"I think that's a great idea," said Charlene, making some notes on her clipboard. "Way to go, Greenview girls! Faith, are you sure you've only been doing this a few months?"

I smiled and took in the praise. I was finally starting to find solid footing on this squad — and I wasn't going to let anyone bring me down!

chapter 8

By the time dinner rolled around, I was starving and ready to chow down — even on mystery meat! Even though it didn't seem possible, Day Two had been even more action-packed than Day One.

After the stunt workshop, we'd taken on a full afternoon of jump, dance, and cheer classes. Then we'd had a private practice session with Coach A and Charlene in order to polish our routine for the big Camp Champs competition the next day. And after that? Our daily eval, where we nailed down — wait for it — a Superior ribbon. *Awesome!*

CAMP EVALUATION

DATE: Day two	SQUAD: Greenview Middle

OVERALL PERFORMANCE

1. Entrance   ④ 3 2 1
2. Spirit   ④ 3 2 1
3. Use of signs   ④ 3 2 1
4. Jumps   ④ 3 2 1
5. Tumbling   ④ 3 2 1
6. Smiles   ④ 3 2 1
7. Voices   ④ 3 2 1
8. Dancing   ④ 3 2 1

Performance section total: _32_

Cheers/stunts section total: _21_

Final total: ___53___

Comments: Great Work!

Continue to work on stunting and you will nail it!

CHEERS/STUNTS

1. Sharp motions   ④ 3 2 1
2. Climbing technique   4 ③ 2 1
3. Timing   ④ 3 2 1
4. Formation   4 ③ 2 1
5. Knowledge of   ④ 3 2 1
   material
6. Perfection of   4 ③ 2 1
   stunts

RATING CHART

50-56 points: Superior

36-49 points: Excellent

28-35 points: Outstanding

14-27 points: Good

"I'm so excited that we're putting the new lib stunt into the Camp Champs routine," said Brooke, putting her tray on the table and sitting down with the rest of us.

"Yeah, I can't wait to learn how to do it," said Gaby, twirling some pasta around her fork. "You guys better teach us when we get back!"

"Oh, we will," said Brooke. "We'll be the sweet ladies of liberty!"

She and Gaby giggled uncontrollably, and Gaby held her fork up in a **Statue of Liberty*** pose.

The discussion was lively as everyone wolfed down their food. Even Ella seemed to be in a great mood, so I assumed the coast was clear and all was forgotten . . . until it wasn't.

"Hey Faith, heard you were totally rocking it out in stunt class today," said Ella. "I guess you're finally getting the hang of this whole cheerleading thing."

"I guess you could say that," I said slowly. What was she getting at?

"Then I'm sure you won't have a problem with the dare I came up with," she said, exchanging a smirk with Kacey.

Great. She was determined to get me. That was clear. I didn't know what to say, so I stayed silent. Hopefully, it would be something easy, and we could move past this.

〜〜〜〜〜

* Speaking of the Statue of Liberty, that's another one of my bucket list hopes. I want to go all the way up to the crown. They limit the number of people who can go up there, so I guess it will take some planning. Maybe I'll hit the Statue on the same trip as my Macy's parade adventure!

"So I dare you to stand up on this table right now and lead the whole cafeteria in the 'Boom-Chicka-Boom' song," said Ella. "And you have to get everyone to sing along."

I was mortified at the mere thought of it. There were hundreds of girls in the cafeteria, and being the sole center of their attention scared me to death! My face turned beet red, and I felt completely frozen. Suddenly, I wasn't hungry anymore.

I turned to Gaby helplessly, but she just shrugged her shoulders and made a face. She probably knew Ella wasn't going to back down!

"You're not going to punk out twice, are you?" asked Ella.

"Yeah," said Kacey. "Everyone on the team had to do something like this when they were new. Consider this your **initiation***!"

---

* An initiation is like a ceremony that makes a person a member of a group. In some groups, it seems like initiation has become another word for torture. An initiation should help girls bond with the group. A slumber party, makeovers, an afternoon of games . . . these are appropriate ways to initiate the new girl!

"Faith! Faith! Faith!" All the Greenview girls started chanting again, and people started looking at our table curiously. I was in a complete panic! Most cheerleaders would probably get on the table and do it no problem. In fact, they'd probably ham it up. But for me, it felt like a death sentence.

"Faith! Faith! Faith!" The chanting continued, and I suddenly felt like I couldn't breathe. I pushed my chair back and ran away from the table as fast as I could.

"I knew she wasn't cheerleader material," I heard Ella huff in the distance. I flung open the doors and continued running full-speed across the quad until I got to the dorm. I wasted no time going straight to Coach A's room.

"Coach, I need your phone," I sobbed.

"Faith, are you all right?" asked Coach, alarmed. I just shook my head. I couldn't even get words out, I was crying so hard.

"Try to tell me what's wrong, and then you can borrow my phone," she said.

I started crying harder. "I just want to talk to my mom,"
I wailed.

"Okay, okay. Stay here, and I'll go take a walk. You can
borrow my phone, but don't go anywhere, okay? I want to
talk to you afterward." I nodded as she handed me her cell.
Coach A could be okay sometimes.

I dialed my home phone as fast as my fingers could fly.
My brother Stevie answered, and he started to tease me as
usual. But once he heard my voice, he ran to get my mom.

"What's wrong, sweetheart?" asked my mom.
I could tell she was really worried.

I tried to speak between jagged sobs. "I just feel totally
out of place here! Everyone is so outgoing, and I'm out of my
league," I said sadly, trying to catch my breath. "And Ella's out
to get me!"

"What? Slow down," said my mom, and I told her the
whole story. I finished by asking her if she could come get me
that night instead of in the morning.

"Oh, honey, you know I will if you really need me to, but try to calm down and think about it for a bit," said Mom. "You've been looking forward to this all summer, and I hate to see one person ruin the whole experience for you."

By the time we hung up, she'd managed to talk me into staying, but I still wasn't very happy about it. In fact, all I wanted to do was disappear and forget the whole thing ever happened. I started to get up to go to my room when Coach A appeared in the doorway. By the look on her face, I could tell she'd heard what happened.

"Faith, please know that Ella's behavior is unacceptable. She will be made aware of that," said Coach sternly. "I do not allow bullying or peer pressure of any kind on my squad."

"Thanks, Coach, but please don't say anything to her," I pleaded, drying my eyes. "It'll only make it worse. Plus, maybe she's right. If I can't even perform in front of the girls at camp, what makes me think I'll be able to perform at games and stuff?"

"Faith, we need you on this squad," said Coach. "You've become a really strong asset, and you've already grown so much as a performer. Don't you dare go anywhere."

It was too much to process all at once. "Right now, I just want to sleep," I told her. "Is it okay if I skip the night activities?" There was supposed to be a jump contest and a dance party, but I had no desire to show my face or see anyone.

"Usually I don't let anyone out of it unless they're sick, but I'll make an exception this once," said Coach. "Go get some rest." And I headed back to my room to try and sleep off the sadness.

When I woke up early the next morning, I had a "Did that really happen?" moment. I rolled over to see if Gaby was awake yet, but she wasn't in her bed. *Oh great,* I thought. Gaby's probably embarrassed to be roommates with the camp crybaby. I buried my head under the pillow, wishing I was anywhere but there.

Then I heard Brooke's voice trailing down the hall.

"Do you think she's awake yet?" I wondered if they were talking about me.

I didn't have to wonder for long.

Brooke, Gaby, and Lissa walked into the room. Brooke was carrying a breakfast tray of pancakes, sausage, and OJ. "She's up!" exclaimed Gaby, running over to give me a hug.

Lissa shut the door, and all three of them sat down on my bed. "Faith! We were so worried last night, but by the time we came back, you were sound asleep and we didn't want to wake you," said Brooke, placing the tray on my lap.

> ## How to Cheer Up a Friend
>
> Is your friend feeling down? Here are a few more ways to cheer her up.
>
> - Give her flowers
> - Help her with her homework or plan a fun study night
> - Meet up at the mall and then surprise her with two movie tickets
> - Loan her your favorite sweater
> - Ask her if she wants to talk... and then be sure to listen

"Thanks, guys," I said, feeling a smidge better. "That was quite a scene, wasn't it?"

"Oh, you missed the best part," said Lissa. "So we didn't get a spirit stick last night, and Ella threw a total fit, saying that it was probably because we didn't have our whole team there —" I cringed at the sound of Ella's name and the thought of Greenview losing awards because of me.

"But then Charlene overheard and told her it was all because of her bad sportsmanship!" said Gaby, laughing. "It was a total 'oh snap!' moment."

"No way," I said. Maybe Ella really was in the wrong with what she did.

"Oh yeah, and you don't even want to hear how Coach reamed her," chimed in Lissa. "She made her sit on the sidelines during the dance party."

"Great, she probably hates me even more now," I moaned, taking a big bite of pancakes. I suddenly realized I was starving. I'd barely eaten any dinner the night before!

"So what?" said Brooke. "Believe me, she'll come around when she sees everyone is on your side."

"I hope you're right," I said, unconvinced. "What else did I miss?"

"Well, the dance party was super fun, and Trina came in second place in the jumping contest!" Gaby said. The three of them filled me in on everything I missed. I was a little bummed that I'd have to wait until next year to take part in these camp traditions — if I even tried out again, that is.

As if reading my mind, Brooke said, "You're up for competing this morning, right? We really need you."

I stared at my cheer uniform hanging on the outside of the closet. Gaby followed my glance and started to tease me. "It's calling your name! Faiiiiiiiith, I need you . . . you must wear me today!"

The three of them started tickle-torturing me until I was forced to relent. "Okay, okay!" I said. I giggled and gestured surrender. "You make it hard to say no."

Lissa and Brooke headed back to their room to get ready, and I managed to finish my breakfast and do the same. After I got my uniform on, Gaby even did my makeup for me! It was so fun to have a bestie to get ready with.

"Wow, you even let me wear your green glitter eye shadow," I joked. "Now I know you feel sorry for me."

"It's yours anytime," said Gaby, putting the finishing touches on my mascara. "You wear it well, friend!"

I looked in the mirror. My hair was up in a high ponytail with ringlet curls and a big gold bow. Gaby had done my stage makeup perfectly. And, of course, the uniform: a sleeveless blue shell top with red stripes across the ribs and "Greenview" written in cursive script. The bottom was a pleated blue and red miniskirt. Looking at my reflection, there was no doubt about it: A cheerleader was staring back at me. Gaby's words meant more than she knew.

"Thanks," I whispered, and I was immediately glad they'd talked me into giving it a go. I wasn't looking forward to facing Ella, but I owed it to myself — and the girls — to try.

CHEER!
Yell!
FLY!
CHEER!
Cheer!
CHANT!
Yell!
SPIRIT!
CHEER!
Cheer!
CHEER!
Cheer!
YELL!
Cheer!
CHANT!
CHEER!
FLY!
CHEER!
CHANT!
Cheer!
FLY!
Cheer!
FLY!

Chapter 10

The morning flew by, and before I knew it, it was time for the Camp Champs competition to begin. My emotions were a jumble. I was still nervous about facing Ella, and I was totally freaked about performing in front of a crowd for the first time. It seemed those butterflies were starting to take up permanent residence in my tummy!

We took a seat on the lawn as the staffers did a little mini-show to kick off the festivities. Ella scooted over to sit next to me, and I stiffened. There would be no escape if she started up with me here.

"Faith, I wanted to tell you that I'm sorry about what happened yesterday," said Ella. "I know I haven't been that welcoming or friendly since you joined the squad, and well . . . I'm sorry about that, too."

Was she for real? I looked around to see if Coach A was within earshot, but she was deep in conversation with another coach.

"Thanks, Ella, I appreciate that," I said slowly. "I guess I just couldn't figure out why you were always on my case."

She started laughing. "Are you kidding? I'm like that with everyone," she said. "But I guess I should have taken it easy on you. I didn't realize you were so . . . **sensitive***."

～～～～～

*sensitive
Main Entry: sen·si·tive \SEN–suh–tiv\
Function: adjective
1 : capable of responding to stimulation
2 a : easily affected or hurt <a sensitive child> b : capable of showing small differences : DELICATE <sensitive scales> c : readily affected by the action of a certain thing <plants sensitive to light>
3 : Faith Higgins

"Yeah, I'm pretty sure a photo of me is in the dictionary next to 'sensitive,'" I said, giggling. "So be a little sensitive to that next time, huh?" I couldn't believe I had just said that, but Ella just nodded and took it in.

"Truce?" she said, and I shook on it.

"Truce," I answered.

I didn't have too much time to process the whole interaction. It was our turn to be on deck. *Just pretend like you're at practice,* I told myself. *Or picture the crowd in their undies or whatever it is people do to overcome stage fright!* The thought of Coach A in granny panties made me giggle, and Brooke looked amused to see me laughing to myself.

"Did I seriously just see Ella Jenkins apologize?" she whispered as we were waiting for the team before us to finish.

"Affirmative," I answered with a grin.

"Wow, Higgins, you've got some serious mojo!" said Brooke. "I've never seen her say 'sorry' to anyone."

"Well, it's a good thing she did," said Lissa. "We need to present a united front out there to win this! So let's do it."

And with that, Troy called our squad name and we ran onto the field, jumping and getting the crowd riled up. (Not too hard to do with fellow cheerleaders!) It was time to debut our Camp Champs routine. We'd paired a dance and tumbling sequence from home with a cheer we'd learned at camp, finishing off with our lovely new liberty extension.

We hit our places, and the first notes of our music filled the air. There was no turning back now! I took a deep breath and launched into the dance choreography. Lissa, Ella, and Kacey began doing their tumbling passes across the formation. It was such a rush seeing the crowd clapping along and shouting their support. My head was spinning with reminders: *Smile, breathe, don't forget this 8-count, point your toes on the toe touch!*

We made it through the dance routine part, and I was definitely on an adrenaline high. After the music ended, it was time to transition to a new formation. At first, when I tried to yell, my throat felt dry, but as we went along, my voice became stronger and more powerful. As we were moving, I passed Gaby, and she gave me a giant smile.

Brooke called the cheer. **"READY?"**

"Set!" we yelled back.

BLUE AND RED
YELL BIG AND BOLD
WHO'S THE BEST?
G-M-S
YELL WITH US!

On the last round, we loaded Brooke into the liberty and lifted her straight up into the air. As we held Brooke up, I was face to face with Sheena and Mackenzie in the stunt. We yelled loudly together on the final **"G-M-S!"** and I felt strong. In front of us, Kacey, Trina, Ella, and Gaby were doing an elevator, and the other four girls knelt in front holding signs that each read "GMS." I couldn't wait to see the video later. I knew we looked awesome!

The crowd clapped and hollered for us, and we ran off the field to grab some Gatorade and water. I couldn't believe I'd made it through my first performance. And not only survived — but thrived! A few of the girls hugged me, and even Ella smiled.

"I guess I was wrong about you, Faith," said Ella. "Maybe you do have what it takes. And here I thought you could never be as fabulous and charismatic as me!"

I narrowed my eyes. Some people never change.

"Kidding!" she said, and even put her arm around me. "Seriously, job well done." Then she walked off to hang out with Kacey.

I walked over to Brooke, Lissa, and Gaby, who were chattering excitedly about our prospects of winning Camp Champs. But funny enough, I felt like I'd already won.

SQUA
CHEER!
Yell! FLY!
SPIRIT!
CHEER!
cheer!
CHANT!
Yell!
SPIRIT!
CHEER!
CHEER!
SQUAD!
Cheer!
CHEER!
CHANT!
HANT!
HEER! FLY! CHEER!
HANT!
ER! CHEER! SQUAD!
heer!
YELL!
CHEER!
SQUAD!
CHANT!
SPIRIT!
CHANT!
YELL!
CHEER!
Cheer!
Squad!
Yell!
Cheer!
Cheer!
CHEER!
SPIRIT!
SQUAD!
SPIRIT!
FLY!
Squad!
JUMP!
POM!
ER!
SQU
CHEER!
JUMP!
Ye
ER!
Cheer! S
Che
CHA
QUAD!
Che
CHANT!
FLY!
SPIRIT Jump
CHANT!
FLY!

SPIRIT! SPIRIT!
Cheer!
Chant CHEER!
CHEER! CHANT! SQUAD! CHANT! Yell!
SPIRIT! Squad!
POM!
CHEER!
SQUAD! POM
FLY! Cheer! CHEER!
CHEER! SQUAD! Yell!
CHE SPIRIT! JUMP!
CHEER! SQUAD! FLY! CHEER! JUMP!
er! Cheer! Cheer! SQUAD!
YELL! CHEER!
Cheer! Yell! Cheer!
CHE CHEER! CHANT!
R! SQUAD!
FLY! SPIRI
heer! CHANT!

Glossary

AFFIRMATIVE (uh-FUR-muh-tiv)—expression of agreement or a statement that something is true

BEFRIENDED (be-FREND-id)—made friends with someone

CHARISMATIC (ka-riz-MAT-ik)—having a special charm that draws people in

CONTAGIOUS (kuhn-TAY-juhss)—tending to spread from person to person

DEMONSTRATE (DEM-uhn-strate)—to show other people how to do something

EXTROVERTED (EX-struh-vert-ed)—outgoing, lively, and talkative

HUMILIATE (hyoo-MIL-ee-ate)—to make someone look or feel foolish or embarrassed

INTERPRETATIONS (in-tur-prih-TAY-shunz)—unique ways of presenting a dance or another form of art

MORTIFIED (MORT-uh-fied)—very embarrassed

OBLIVIOUS (uh-BLIV-ee-us)—not aware

POTENTIAL (puh-TEN-shuhl)—what you are capable of achieving

REASSURANCE (ree-uh-SHUR-uhns)—restored confidence or courage

SOLIDARITY (sol-uh-DARE-uh-tee)—unity; agreement among a group of people that they will work together to reach a goal

SOPHISTICATED (suh-FISS-tuh-kay-tid)—knowing a lot about the world

SPECTATOR (SPEK-tay-tur)—someone who watches an event and does not participate in it

Cheer!

Tell me the truth...

I know that I can be a little too shy and sensitive sometimes, and maybe that makes me sort of weird. But I'm trying to come out of my shell . . . I mean, I went out for cheerleading! What do you think? Did I handle these situations right?

* I was mortified when Ella pointed out that I needed a large uniform. Do you think I did the right thing by ignoring her? Should I have said something?

* I was so confused the first few hours of camp. Was there anything I could have done to feel more comfortable there? What do you do in those sorts of situations?

* Coach A made it sound like Ella was bullying me, but I didn't even realize that was what she was doing. Do you agree with Coach A? What's the best way to deal with a bully?

The online forums of my favorite cheer magazines have been my go-to place to post questions about the sport. Some of the questions are about school, friends, even boys. So I can probably answer a question or two. Help me write answers to these great questions!

I'm the biggest one!

posted 7 hours ago by bigspirit

I am the biggest girl on my squad. I am not overweight or anything. I just happen to be taller than everyone else and my build is pretty muscular. I just wish I didn't feel like I stuck out so much. How can I get comfortable in my own skin?

They are making me move!

posted 3 days ago by pomloser

My parents are making me move after I finally made my goal of becoming cheer captain. And now I won't even be able to cheer at my new school, since it will be in the middle of the season. I am SO mad at my parents. What should I do?

which cheerleader are you?

Quiz: Are you Brooke, Faith, Gaby, or Lissa? Take this fun quiz to find out which cheerleader you're most like.

1. You forget your homework. You:

A. Make sure to talk to the teacher about it privately. You don't want to draw attention to yourself in class.

B. Turn it in the next day, and ask for an opportunity for extra credit so you can make up missed points.

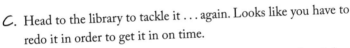

C. Head to the library to tackle it . . . again. Looks like you have to redo it in order to get it in on time.

D. Don't realize it until it's time to hand it in, so you make a joke, give a grin, and promise the teacher you'll turn it in tomorrow.

2. The school play is coming up. You:

A. Volunteer to be a stagehand. You like being involved, but you aren't going to get up in front of anyone.

B. Have no plans to try out. You like to stick to physical extracurriculars.

C. Would love to try out, but will it fit into your busy schedule?

D. Plan to try out. After all, you love to meet new people!

3. You have a free afternoon. You:

A. Paint in your room. You like to spend time by yourself to rejuvenate.

B. Head out for a hike. It will be good exercise.

C. Start with some study time, go on a bike ride, and then make plans for the party you are hosting.

D. Work on some new choreography. There are some new dance steps you have been dying to add to the school song routine.

4. Cheerleading tryouts are next week. How do you feel?

A. Uncertain. Cheerleading sounds fun, but the limelight is a little too hot for you.

B. You can't wait. You're going to nail that new tumbling pass.

C. Awesome! After tryouts, you'll be one step closer to becoming captain.

D. Pretty excited . . . you'll be back with your girls, and making new friends, too.

Quiz continues on the next page.

5. Your favorite thing about cheerleading is:

A. Learning a new skill. You had no idea you had it in you.

B. Working toward a common goal, like new uniforms or fees.

C. Helping others learn the cheers and dances so they can do their best.

D. Making posters and goody bags for the teams. It's fun to chat and hang out as we're working.

6. What role do you fill on the squad?

A. New girl — I'm still figuring it out.

B. Treasurer — I can tell you how much money we have (or need).

C. Leader — I like to make sure everyone is in the know.

D. Social butterfly — I see to it that cheerleading is fun for everyone!

7. My family . . .

A. Has a lot of fun coming up with crazy things to do together.

B. Is small, but tight. I can count on my mom for anything.

C. Is proud of me. They encourage me to work hard and be my best.

D. Is loud and fun! It's bound to be, with all those siblings around.

8. when I'm with my friends, you can be sure I:

A. Will be a good listener. And if the moment arises, I'll get a laugh or two.

B. Will tell people exactly what's on my mind. I'm sassy like that.

C. Have organized an activity for us. I like making sure everyone is having fun!

D. Will be happy and carefree. And if someone has a fashion crisis, I'll be solving it.

If you chose:

----> Mostly A — You are Faith. You may be shy, but when you're with your friends or family, you shine with your sweetness and fun sense of humor.

----> Mostly B — You are Lissa. You work hard to meet your goals. Best of all, your friends know they can count on you to be honest and supportive.

----> Mostly C — You are Brooke. You like to be in charge, and you're good at it. If a friend or teammate comes to you, she knows that you'll be happy to help her.

----> Mostly D — You are Gaby. You make friends easily and can be counted on to ease the mood. Friends appreciate your spunky style and sheer silliness.

A note from Faith...

When I first joined the team, it felt like I had moved to Paris after only one or two years of French class. Sure, I understood some of what was said around me, but a lot of the time, I was left standing in a fog. So I found some books to help me out. Here is a section from _Cheer Basics: Rules to Cheer By_ that was super helpful.

Wendy Wannabe wonders, "What's the difference between . . ."

- **A cheer and a chant?** Repeated three times, a chant is a catchy set of sentences designed for crowd participation. Cheers are longer and often feature signs or stunting.

- **A clap and a clasp?** Claps are tight with flat palms. Clasps are louder and stronger, with hands gripping each other. Both create rhythm and dramatic pauses in cheers.

Wendy Wannabe wonders, "Are all cheer squads the same?"

Far from it. Sports squads cheer on the sidelines, while competition squads focus on winning cheer competitions. All-star squads unite cheerleaders from different schools to compete together on a large athletic team. All three types can be either all-girl or a mix of boys *and* girls.

Wendy Wannabe wonders, "What on earth is . . ."

- **A spirit stick?** Spirit sticks are awarded at camp to the most eager and loyal cheerleaders. Legend has it that spirit sticks should never touch the ground, for fear of bad luck in competition.

- **A formation?** Formations are shapes that show cheerleaders where to stand during routines, like a "V" or straight line. The coach decides placement by skill and height.

- **A peel-off?** A peel-off is a visual effect. Remember the time your music teacher made you sing in rounds? It's a bit like that. All cheerleaders do the same movements at different times. The visual effect looks like a wave.

* Excerpted from *Cheer Basics: Rules to Cheer By,* by Jen Jones, published by Capstone Press in 2006.

Meet the Author:
Jen Jones

Author Jen Jones brings a true love of cheerleading to her Team Cheer series. Here's what she has to say about the series, cheerleading, and reading.

Q. What is your own cheer experience?
A. I absolutely love cheerleading! I cheered from fifth grade until senior year of high school, and went on to cheer for a semi-pro football team in Chicago for several years. I've also coached numerous teams, and I write for a few cheerleading magazines.

Q. Did any of your family members cheer?
A. Some families are into football — mine is into cheerleading! My mom was a coach for close to 20 years, and my sister cheered throughout grade school and high school. My aunt and cousins were also cheerleaders.

Q. Which cheerleader from the series are you most like?
A. I would say I am probably a combination of Gaby and Brooke: Gaby for her outgoing, bubbly nature, and Brooke for her over-achieving, go-getter side. In certain situations, I wish I could channel some of Lissa's feisty fabulousness!

Q. What sort of goals did you have when writing the series?

A. My goals were to create relatable characters that girls couldn't help but like, and also give readers a realistic look at what life on a young competitive cheer squad is like. I want readers to finish the book wanting to be a member of the Greenview Girls!

Q. What kind of reader were you as a kid?

A. I loved to read and often brought home dozens of books every time I went to the library. Whether at the dinner table or in bed, my nose was ALWAYS in a book. Some of my favorite authors were Judy Blume, Lois Duncan, Lois Lowry, Paula Danziger, and Christopher Pike.

Read all of the Team Cheer books

#2-Brooke's Quest for Captain

#3-Lissa and the Fund-Raising Funk

#4-The Competition for Gaby

THE FUN DOESN'T STOP HERE!

DISCOVER MORE AT WWW.CAPSTONEKIDS.COM

☆ Videos & Contests
☆ Games & Puzzles
☆ Friends & Favorites
☆ Authors & Illustrators

Find cool websites and more books like this one at www.facthound.com. Just type in the BOOK ID: 9781434229946 and you're ready to go!

Yell!
FLY!
CHEER!
Cheer!
CHANT!
FLY!
Cheer!
SPIRIT!
CHEER!
Cheer!
CHEER!
YELL!
Cheer!
Cheer!
HANT!
FLY!
CHEER!
FLY!
ANT!
Cheer!
FLY!
POM!
SQUA
CHEER!
Ye
Cheer!
CHAN

SPIRIT!
Cheer!
CHEER!
Yell!
FLY!
JUMP!
POM!
CHEER!
Cheer!
FLY!
Cheer!
CHANT!
SQUAD!
POM!
CHEER!
Yell!
Yell!
SPIR
CHEER!
SQUAD!
SQUAD!
Cheer!
SPIRIT!
CHEER!
Cheer!
Cheer!
CHANT!
CHANT!
CHEER!
FLY!
CHANT!